MW00834082

# BIG SUNDAE

## RANDY HORTON

*Artesian* **Press**

P.O. Box 355 Buena Park, CA 90621

# Take Ten Books
# Sports

Other Take Ten Themes:
**Mystery**
**Adventure**
**Disaster**
**Chillers**
**Thrillers**
**Fantasy**

Project Editor:Liz Parker
Assistant Editor: Carol Newell
Cover Illustrator:Marjorie Taylor
Cover Designer: Tony Amaro
Text Illustrator:Fujiko Miller
©2000 Artesian Press

 *Artesian Press*

ISBN 1-58659-03

# Chapter 1

Monty Platt was on a losing streak. Everything had gone wrong in the last two months. He studied all night for his final geometry quiz, then slept through his paper route. He was fired, then he failed the geometry quiz. The soccer team didn't want him, or the football team. The tennis coach said his arms were too short. Life didn't like Monty Platt very much, and he didn't like life. But his parents told him things would get better; parents always say those sorts of things. They sent him to his uncle's house for winter vacation. Uncle Kevin and Aunt Jill were waiting at the airport when he arrived. Unfortunately, his luggage was sent to Tahiti.

Monty liked his relatives well enough. His cousin Jenny had a good sense of humor. But nothing they did could cheer him up. "You just need a little self confidence," said his uncle, as they drove home from the Crosstown Airport. "Do you know how to ski?"

"I went a few times," Monty said. "Until I ran into a ski instructor."

"Great." Uncle Kevin nodded to his wife. "We're going on a little trip tomorrow. You'll see, Monty. You do a few runs successfully and you'll get that confidence back. Failure is just a matter of confidence."

"He's right, honey." Aunt Jill puckered her lips, applying lipstick in the rearview mirror. "Your luck will change in no time at all."

Monty nodded absently. He'd heard this sort of thing before.

It snowed that night. His cousin, Jenny, woke him at six in the morning.

"We're ready to go," she said, tickling his foot.

"Go?" Monty wasn't quite awake yet.

"We're skiing today," she said. "You know how to ski, right? You're not going to embarrass me on the slopes, are you?" Jenny was tough. She skied on the cross-country team for her high school, and was basically more successful than Monty.

"I'm sleeping." Monty pulled the blanket up over his head.

Jenny waited a moment in silence. Then she yanked off the blanket and dragged Monty out by his feet. "We're leaving in ten minutes," she said. "Dad wants you to be happy, and I want Dad to be happy. Dad wants you to ski, so you're going to ski. And don't screw up."

"I screw everything up. I'm a teen failure."

Jenny pulled him into the kitchen

where Aunt Jill had whipped up a batch of her famous scrambled eggs. Then she sat him down at the table. "Eat fast," she said, checking her watch. "In ten minutes you'd better be waiting in the back of Dad's car—or else." There was a very determined look in her eyes. Monty nodded and reached for his fork.

Exactly ten minutes later, the Underdall family drove to Mount Maudlin.

There was only one large mountain near Crosstown, but it was huge. Mount Maudlin created the town, actually. Miners in the late eighteen hundreds settled there to look for gold. What they found was copper ore. Mining copper wasn't as glamorous, but it made a nice living for those who decided to stay. The Maudlin Mining Company owned the southern edge of the mountain. A ski lodge was built to the north.

Thirty minutes after they arrived, Monty rode up the lift next to Jenny. There weren't many people out, despite fresh snow. "I forgot about the annual Four-H Club tractor pull today." Jenny pointed to a large dirt arena near the edge of town. "All the cool people are over there. So don't worry about embarrassing me. You can screw up as much as you want."

The lift moved on over the giant 'M' carved into the mountain. "You can see that from anywhere in Crosstown," Jenny said. "The Maudlin family owns everything here, even the mountain."

"They must be rich." Monty stared down the slope. It would be a long way to roll.

"Rich, powerful, beautiful. Laura Maudlin is about your age. She's been chosen Miss Copper Ore two years running."

The ski lift topped the mountain

and Monty promptly fell onto his face in the snow. Jenny lifted him up, and together they made their way to the learner's slope.

"You waxed the skis?" asked Jenny. "And you tuned the edges?"

"Everything." Monty checked his bindings and turned to watch Aunt Jill and Uncle Kevin slalom down the expert slope. They wore bright neon-orange ski suits. Monty wore his Army surplus jacket, and his rental skis were chipped and worn; it looked like a German shepherd had been gnawing on the ends.

"Just do what I told you and everything should be all right." Jenny looked him in the eye. "And don't go beyond the ropes, right?"

"Look," Monty groaned. "Don't treat me like an idiot. I know all this stuff; I just have trouble making it work."

"Fine. It's your funeral, pal." Jenny

pushed off over the snow. Monty watched her zoom across to the expert side. She wasn't about to waste her time on the learner's slope.

The rest of the Underdalls would be busy for a while, so Monty figured he'd better practice a few moves before he committed himself. Stopping had always been his biggest problem. He pushed off sideways over the ridge. Then he turned his skis in toward each other until the tips crossed. It was a beginner's move—the snowplow. Experienced skiers wouldn't be caught dead using a move like that.

Monty pushed forward over a path that lead back to the learner's hill. So many people had skied down this path it had been flattened down to ice. The ice kept him moving at a fast pace.

Then the path swerved left, away from the slopes.

Monty looked back. The learner's hill was nowhere to be seen, and the ice path became steeper and steeper. It swerved around a clump of trees and Monty nearly lost his balance. He was in the middle of the forest now, sliding down a central path that led him away from the safe northern hill.

The path was too slick to try a snowplow. The only way he could stop was to throw himself off the trail. But trees were everywhere. If he dove sideways, off the path, he'd jump right into a tree. Monty had never been skiing this fast; even the Underdalls hadn't been skiing this fast. The wind whistled in his ears. The sound of his skis on the ice was all he could hear.

He sailed down past some rope laying in the snow by a pine tree. It had blocked off the trail at one time, but someone had unhooked it. In an instant the rope was behind him and out of sight. Monty prayed for a snow drift to fall into, anything to slow him down. It was all he could do to hold his balance and avoid the trees.

He hit a lump of ice and flew a foot into the air before his skis slapped back down on the trail. Branches whipped his face. Monty wiped his eyes then looked out to see the whole expanse of Mount Maudlin. He was skiing down the wrong side.

There was a yellow rope across the path ahead. Monty reached out to grab it, but it was just a plastic police banner. It wrapped around his body and fluttered out behind him like a twenty foot streamer. Monty looked down at his chest to read the words: Avalanche Danger! Do Not Cross Barricade!

Then he hit the steep part.

The mountain dropped off at a sixty-degree angle. Monty's skis skittered on the edge for a moment before he shot down into the drop. He couldn't imagine how fast he must be going—fifty, sixty miles an hour. He could barely keep his eyes open. No more than one hundred yards ahead, he saw the ragged edge of an open quarry pit. The cliff dropped off so far he couldn't see the bottom.

If Monty could have taken the time to think, he would have thought of the advice his Uncle had given him: "Failure," he said, "is only a matter of confidence."

And it was true. Monty looked down at the giant open quarry that lay before him, quite confident of his upcoming failure. He only hoped it wouldn't be his last.

# Chapter 2

Scoutmaster David and his troop of scouts were standing in the quarry investigating mineral deposits as Monty zoomed past. They watched him ski along the rim for a few yards, then swoop down into the quarry.

"Look, boys." Scoutmaster David pointed. "He must be going fifty miles an hour."

"Can we do that?" asked little Eric, looking up from a large piece of copper ore.

"No, what he's doing is very dangerous. There's a cliff down there—over a hundred foot drop." Scoutmaster David pointed to the bottom of the hill. "But we can follow him down. I think this is the perfect time to begin our study of first aid techniques."

As the scouts worked their way to the foot of the trail, the Underdall family stood on the other side of the mountain, eyeing the slopes for any sign of Monty. "He screwed up," said Jenny. "I knew it."

"Do you think we'd better call the ski patrol?" Aunt Jill asked, touching up her makeup.

Uncle Kevin nodded, frowning. "Knowing that boy, we'd better call the hospital."

Meanwhile, Monty was utterly terrified. The surface of the quarry slope had partially iced over, and his skis were moving so fast they'd begun to vibrate. His legs shook violently and his knees felt like they were ready to give. He knew if he fell over now, at this speed, he'd surely break a leg.

And the brink of the quarry pit lay open before him, like the edge of the world.

Monty leaned heavily on his right leg, hoping to turn right, away from the open pit. He was moving so fast, it didn't have much of an effect. But he leaned hard, and slowly he began to turn. The edge of the pit was only ten feet away, his skis flung snow over the drop as he swerved right—right over another cliff.

Suddenly he wasn't on snow anymore. There was a long metal chute underneath him, and it rattled like thunder as he shot down the length of it. The chute was built like a giant slide on the edge of the mountain. On either side there was nothing but air.

Then the chute ended. The metal rattling stopped. His knees stopped shaking, and there was nothing but the sound of wind in his ears. He felt just like a bird, flying through the air. Except of course that birds have wings, and birds never have to worry about falling to their deaths on the second day of winter vacation.

There were people down below. It looked like a party of some sort. Monty hoped he wouldn't land on anyone special.

At the bottom of the mountain, Max Maudlin, copper tycoon and all around rich businessman, hugged his daughter Laura as tightly as he could. "Happy birthday dear," he said, pointing to the 1962 Mustang convertible he'd had rebuilt for her. "You're the best daughter I've ever had."

"I'm the only daughter you've ever had," said Laura, taking the keys. "But I am the best, I'll have to agree." She was joking, but only to a certain extent. "This is the best birthday party ever. I love you, Daddy." Laura hugged him back, looking over Mr. Maudlin's shoulder to see Monty skiing down the hill above them, flying into the air.

"And you hired a stunt man for my

birthday, too!"

Mr. Maudlin turned around just as Monty sailed over their heads, the yellow police banner fluttering in the wind behind him. "My God!" he exclaimed, "get that on video!" Mr. Maudlin pointed to the cameraman he'd hired to record his daughter's birthday.

"Got it," said the cameraman. "I can sell this to the local news for big bucks."

They watched as Monty hit the ground. Snow flew up in a cloud, but Monty kept moving, over the snow, finally coming to a halt about a hundred yards away.

Monty looked down at his body, amazed that everything was still in place. There were no broken bones, no contusions, no fractures, no concussions ... nothing. He hadn't even torn his jacket. Something was terribly, terribly wrong.

He turned to see about fifty people running toward him. They were screaming, and for a moment he thought he was in some kind of trouble. But then an older girl grabbed Monty around the neck and hugged him tight.

"You made this the best birthday party I've ever had!" she said, rubbing her nose against his cheek. "Whoever you are, I can't thank you enough!"

People were shaking his hands, two at a time. A large well-dressed man patted him on the back. "Good work, son," he said, slipping a Havana cigar into Monty's front pocket.

"But I don't smoke," said Monty.

"Doesn't matter," said Mr. Maudlin, "it's expensive."

They brought Monty over to the girl's birthday party and sat him down at a huge wooden picnic table. The girl's name was Laura, and though she didn't seem to have a very long attention span, Monty was all she could talk about. "I can't believe how good you are," she said. "Someone so young." She leaned forward, touching his knee for support. "You're good enough to compete in the Olympics."

"I just did what I had to do," Monty said, through a mouthful of birthday cake. "I guess skiing comes naturally to me."

The scout troop soon arrived, and they joined in the festivities, too. "You're going to be on the local news," said the cameraman. "I've got everything on film. You'll be a city-wide hero."

Laura Maudlin stood, her hands on Monty's shoulders. "And if you're going to be a hero in this city, you have to see what it looks like. I'll drive you around tonight in my new car." Her father nodded, smiling as the cameraman filmed them all. "I just love athletes," Laura whispered as the scouts began to cheer.

Monty couldn't stop smiling; his cheeks hurt. He waved to the cameraman, his arm around Laura, and ate so much chocolate cake he thought he might be sick. Then, through the crowd, he saw his aunt and uncle waving cheerfully. Monty pulled away from Laura for a moment, pushing through the crowd toward them—just as his cousin Jenny grabbed him by the arm.

"Did you hear what happened?" Monty said, hugging her.

"You nearly killed yourself," Jenny said. "What's the big deal?"

"No, I skied off a cliff. Perfectly. I'm an expert." Monty laughed and ran to tell Uncle Kevin.

Jenny shook her head. It didn't look good. Monty might have survived, but she was sure that unless he took himself a little less seriously, the boy was in for the biggest fall of all.

# Chapter 3

"It was just an accident," Jenny said, handing Monty his tie. "You skied off a cliff, and by a one-in-a-million chance, you happened to survive."

"There are no accidents." Monty eyed himself in the mirror. "I've been unlucky all my life; don't you think it's fair that I got lucky at something?"

"But you can't just be good at skiing. You have to practice."

Monty nodded absently, walking out the door. "So I'll practice. We'll go skiing again next week." Quite simply, he was more concerned about Laura Maudlin than skiing. This was the first time anyone had ever asked him out on a date.

Laura lived in Crosstown's richest neighborhood; he had to take a bus there. The house was four stories high, and carried on so far back Monty had no idea how many rooms it might have. He knocked for a full minute before the butler let him in.

Monty followed the butler through two hallways and a sitting room before he found Mr. Maudlin, sitting by himself before a roaring fire.

"Howdy, son!" Mr. Maudlin sat Monty down in a large leather chair. "Laura will be down in a moment. You'll have to talk loud; this fire makes so much noise, I can't hear a thing!"

"Wonderful house!" shouted Monty.

"Fine, I'm fine." Mr. Maudlin reached over to turn down the fireplace. It was powered by tiny gas jets from somewhere underneath. "But most importantly, boy, how are you?"

The butler poured Monty a cola as Mr. Maudlin dragged his chair up close. "I don't even have to ask that," he said, speaking a few inches from Monty's face. "I can see it myself; you're about as fine as a young man can be. You like to ski, don't you?"

"Sure," said Monty.

"You like to ski quite a bit, I'll wager."

Monty took a long drink of his cola, wondering if he should say 'sure' once more.

"I'll bet," said Mr. Maudlin, "You like to ski so much you'd be willing to do another little jump like the one you performed this morning." The old man's eyebrows arched, throwing spiky shadows over the weathered folds of skin along his forehead. "I'll pay you, of course."

"But ..."

"Lots and lots of money," said Mr. Maudlin. "More money that it would take to date my daughter on a regular basis."

Suddenly, there was a squeal from the stairway. Monty turned to see Laura Maudlin, wearing an incredibly bright, red outfit. "He's going to do it, Daddy?" she asked.

"He's still bargaining on the price," said Mr. Maudlin. "You've got a tough little boyfriend here."

Laura scampered over, hugging Monty tightly around the neck. "Oh, do say you'll do it. I have to see you jump off that mountain again. Please?"

Monty choked on his cola, picturing the edge of the quarry, and the sixty foot drop. "Why?" he said finally, catching his breath. "I don't understand."

"Ice cream." Mr. Maudlin grinned.

"Ice cream?"

"Daddy's going to open up a new ice cream store in Crosstown. The biggest."

"Ice Cream Heaven," said Mr. Maudlin. "That's the name. What do you think?"

"But you want me to jump off a cliff?" Monty shrugged. The butler took his empty cola and replaced it with another.

"On opening day I'm going to throw a little celebration." Mr. Maudlin stood, spreading his arms wide. "Right where we were today. Picture this: a band playing, free ice cream for the kids. I know it's cold out, but people will eat anything if it's free." He pulled Monty to his feet, pointing to an imaginary mountain in the distance. "Then, at the top of Mount Maudlin, you ski down the slope, off a giant metal spoon."

"You mean that mining sluice?"

"We'll make it look like a spoon," said Mr. Maudlin. "Anyway, you ski down, off the spoon, and land in a giant ice cream sundae!"

"We'll make one out of snow," said Laura. "It was my idea."

"People will lap it up. What do you say?"

Laura hugged him tightly. Monty couldn't breathe. He pictured himself back on that mountain, full of terror, completely unsure if he might live or die as he zoomed off the edge of the cliff.

"Lots of money," said Mr. Maudlin.

"Please, Monty." Laura hugged him even tighter.

Monty grew dizzy. He reached for his cola, head spinning. Jumping off that cliff was definitely not something he needed to try again, but somewhere, in the distance between his hand and that frosted glass, he heard himself saying—yes.

Laura sped out of the Maudlin driveway, exceeding the speed limit in under three seconds. "I'm taking you out to dinner," she said simply. "But first I want to show you around."

They drove down the main drag,

Laura waving to nearly every other vehicle on the road. It was as if the car itself knew where they were going; Laura certainly didn't seem to be paying any attention. "I know everyone in Crosstown," she said, casually driving through a red light. "And if I don't know them, they don't exist."

"You must be popular." Monty watched the road, ready to grab the wheel should the need arise.

"It's fun," she said. "But being popular is a responsibility too. I have to let everyone know what's good, what's bad, what's pretty ... and speaking of what's ugly, look at that hag in the black dress!" Laura pointed out the window as she veered into a parking lot.

It was Jenny, in her waitress uniform, heading into work.

"That's my cousin," said Monty. "She has to wear that uniform; she's a waitress."

"Of course, some people have to work." Laura laughed, tickling the hair on the back of his neck. "Forgive me; I don't mean to be cruel."

She parked the car and hopped out. "I promise, if she's our waitress tonight, I'll give her a big, big tip." Monty nodded, smiling. Laura never really seemed to be serious, but then she never really seemed to be joking either. He took her hand, and together they headed into Beijing's Wok of Fame, the most expensive Chinese restaurant in Crosstown. It was the only Chinese restaurant in Crosstown, but this did nothing to blemish its fine reputation.

"Order anything you want," said Laura, as Monty held the door for her. "Anyone who can ski like you do deserves the best."

"You know, I was thinking about that jump ..." The Chinese hostess greeted Laura warmly and led them to the best table in the house. "I was thinking, Laura, that it might not be such a good idea."

Laura didn't hear him; she was busy waving to a blonde couple across the room. "Did you see this boy on the news?" she said to another group as they sat down. "He's going off the mountain again next week! God's gift to skiing."

Monty cleared his throat as Jenny stepped up with a pair of menus. He smiled wanly. "Hi, Jenny."

"Howdy, stud." Jenny nodded and walked away.

"You're going to be so famous after this next jump."

Laura ignored the menu, reaching over the table to grab his hands in her own. She grinned at him over the bowl of fried noodles that formed the table's centerpiece. "I am in awe of your athletic ability."

"You know, I'm really not that good," he said. "I don't think …"

"Posh." Laura shook back her silky red hair. "Would I be here with you now if you weren't? I don't hang out with just anyone. If you weren't the best skier in Crosstown I'd be over there right now." She nodded to a table near the rear of the restaurant where a large, square-jawed boy sat, eating soup with one of the most beautiful girls he'd ever seen. "If I said the word," Laura winked, "that girl would be out the door before she swallowed another won ton."

Monty knew she was telling the truth.

"That boy has always loved me," she said. "I broke his heart about a month ago."

They talked about skiing, and then Laura talked about how much she loved men who skied, and then Monty told her what it was like to ski off Maudlin Mountain. After dinner they sat together, enjoying a final cup of jasmine tea. Jenny brought the check, handing them each a fortune cookie.

"Tell me what yours says." Laura bit into her cookie.

Monty cracked his cookie open. Inside, there was the expected slip of paper. But something was different about it; the fortune had been written in ball point pen. It said: He who leaps into the unknown may break both of his legs.

Monty stared back to the rear of the restaurant where Jenny stood, watching him grimly. It was true. If he was going to make that jump and survive, Monty would need some help, and fast.

Under the table, Laura rubbed his leg with her toe.

# Chapter 4

He'd been practicing for two days and only seemed to get worse. Jenny sat on a stump, filing her nails. Monty sat in the snow, filing his skis. "You have to do the edges evenly," she said, staring at her cuticles.

"I know." Monty reached for the wax.

"And don't forget to wax them afterwards."

"Tell me something I don't know," he muttered.

Jenny checked his binding, nodded brusquely, and took off down the intermediate slope. She yelled back over her shoulder, "Just do exactly what I do."

Monty watched Jenny slalom

around a large rock, snow whipping up in her path. It was the third time he'd tried to slalom that rock. The first time he plowed right into it, and the second time he'd plowed right into it.

Monty pushed off with his poles and made for the rock. He heard Jenny's voice in his head: "Keep control of your skis. Don't let your skis take control of you." It almost worked; he managed to swerve away at the last second. But on the return, Monty skidded sideways, lost a ski, and toppled into a snow bank. On his back, Monty looked up from inside the snow cave he'd created. Jenny's face suddenly came into view.

"Your skis took control of you," she said. "Try it again."

By lunchtime he'd managed the basics of rock avoidance. "With luck you might make it to the jump." Jenny handed him one of Aunt Jill's fabulous homemade peanut butter and banana sandwiches. "That's with luck. Without luck, you'll fly off the wrong edge of the quarry and fall to your death. Still want to do it?"

"Of course not," said Monty. "But what other choice do I have?"

"Not to do it." Jenny shrugged, wiping the snow from her legs. "But you like the girl too much, don't you?"

"She likes me." Monty stood, ready to ski. "I know Laura's not the nicest person in the world. It's the fame and popularity too. I want to be popular."

"Well, just remember …" Jenny took off down the hill with a flick of her poles, "dead people are the least popular of all."

He had nightmares that evening. Monty pictured himself skiing down one giant scoop of a monstrous ice cream sundae. Then he hit the hot fudge. Mounds of french vanilla rolled down from above. He woke up sweating and hungry.

The next morning Jenny taught him how to jump.

"The most important thing is to keep loose," she said, at the top of the hill. "Keep your knees bent, your feet together." She pointed with her pole to a tiny mound, about three feet high. "That's a mogul. Ski right over the top of that. We'll see if you know how to land."

"I skied off a cliff and landed pretty well," said Monty.

"Okay," Jenny smiled. "So I won't say another word." In seconds she was half way down the slope, off the mogul, and into the air. Jenny landed perfectly, both skis turning left to stop, a wave of powder flying up in her wake.

Monty pushed off, making straight for the tiny hill. He pictured himself in the air; he pictured the precision of his movement as he flew off the top, his skis leaving the snow at the exact same moment. Then he went off the mogul, one ski up, one ski to the right, and fell right on his back.

"Always keep your skis close together." Jenny stared down at him, shaking her head. "And your knees together. Otherwise you fall on your back and look stupid."

Monty nodded silently. There were only two days left until the big grand opening. Two days left to learn how to ski. And then learn how to jump. And then learn how to land.

Laura picked him up that evening. "Hi, Jen," she said at the door. "I came for your cousin."

Jenny nodded silently and walked back to find Monty.

Meanwhile, Laura helped herself to a diet soda from the Underdall's refrigerator. "Pretty nice spread for a girl who works in a Chinese restaurant," she said, when Jenny and Monty found her in the kitchen.

"My dad is a lawyer." Jenny closed

the refrigerator door. "He defends corporations."

"Well, maybe he knows my father." Laura drained her soda and set in on the kitchen counter. "He *is* a corporation."

Monty took her outside before Miss Maudlin could say any more. They hopped into her Mustang, and she drove straight to the local mall.

"Why are we here?" Monty asked, as she paid three-fifty to have her car parked.

"It's your costume." Laura skipped to the entrance, holding the door for him. "You have to be fitted, of course."

"Fitted?"

"You're the Ice Cream Heaven mascot." She pulled him inside, her arm around his.

"A mascot? That's an animal kept by a sports team."

"Not an animal." She led Monty into a men's clothing design store.

"You're going to be a fruit."

"What?"

"Monty—the wild cherry." Laura motioned to a thin man behind the counter. "It was my idea. You wear a cherry costume when you ski down on top of the giant sundae. It'll look marvelous on film. It's perfect!" Laura became so excited that she turned and kissed him right there in the store.

As their lips met, Monty looked behind her to where the man stood, measuring bright, red, elastic material.

"You'll be a wonderful mascot," Laura said, stepping away. "The best cherry in the whole world."

When he came home that night, Monty threw the cherry outfit onto his bed and went out to the shed behind the house. He pulled Uncle Kevin's skis off the wall and tried them on for size. Then he borrowed Aunt Jill's boots. By the glow of the bug zapper, Monty practiced skiing back and forth across the yard. It was confidence, he told himself. Confidence was all he needed to make the big jump. Confidence and skill.

# Chapter 5

The whole thing just seemed to grow bigger and bigger. Everyone was interested in Monty's big jump. As he practiced the next day, a group of athletically inclined nuns came to watch. They sat on tree stumps beside the slope, applauding each time Monty skied off a mogul or successfully avoided a tree. It was nerve wracking to have those eyes following his every move. Laura wanted to drive by in her snowmobile, but Monty told her to wait for the big event. "It'll be more impressive that way," he said on the phone. "You'll appreciate me just that much more."

He practiced all day and most of the

evening, and by morning every muscle in Monty's body was on fire. Jenny woke him at six o'clock, tickling his feet.

"Time to go to the hospital … er, I mean the ski slope," she said. Monty slid out of bed without a fight. There was still time to practice for a few hours before Mr. Maudlin arrived at the mountain with his camera crew.

Jenny took him to the expert slope. Monty stared down from the top of the mountain. It looked almost as steep as the dangerous side. She gave him a shove, and Monty took off down the hill, picturing that final, climactic jump in his mind. He skied back and forth to slow himself down, and even managed to ski off a tiny mogul before he fell. It was such a peaceful experience, laying on his back in the snow—as if there were no ice cream parlors in the world, or rich, beautiful girls. Monty decided right there, at that moment, that he would lie in the snow for the rest of his life.

Jenny reached down and pulled him to his knees. "Look," she said, pointing down the mountain. "It's time to go. The camera crew just arrived."

By twelve o'clock most of Crosstown had come to the foot of the mountain. Mr. Maudlin set up a huge table with as much free ice cream as anyone could stomach. "Who cares if it's cold outside," he bellowed to the crowd. "It's free!" There were at least a thousand people milling around aimlessly, and in the center of them all stood Laura Maudlin.

She rode the ski lift up, to find Monty still practicing. Laura dragged him down to the festivities. Mr. Maudlin had ordered an Olympic-sized, above-ground pool, and built it right where Monty landed on his first jump. The pool was decorated to look like a porcelain bowl, then filled with snow and some brown foam that looked like fudge. Laura guided Monty to the ski lodge and waited while he climbed into his cherry costume. It was too tight, too bright, and all together too silly looking, but she loved it. Afterward, she coaxed Monty up to the top of the giant sundae, motioning for the crowd to quiet down.

"Here he is," she said through a loudspeaker. "The craziest cherry in history. Monty—the wild cherry!"

He waved, feeling as silly as a party clown.

"And do you see that 'M' up there on the mountain?" It had been painted bright red that morning by two workers. "The M stands for more than just Maudlin today." Laura lifted Monty's left hand over her head in a power salute. "It stands for Monty! The wild cherry!" Cheers rippled through the crowd as Monty was led into the passenger seat of a tiny snowmobile, then driven around the edge of the giant sundae. Finally, as a polka band began to play its version of "Born to be Wild," Monty rode the ski lift up to the top of the jump.

Jenny was waiting for him when he arrived.

"You know you aren't prepared?" she said, following him down the path along the top of the ridge.

"I know." Monty stared at his ski boots.

"Even *you* admit you aren't prepared." She held Monty back by a sleeve. "It's ridiculous. You don't have to prove anything to anyone, Monty."

"They won't like me anymore if I give up now," he said sadly.

"I like you, and *I* know you can't ski." From the foot of the mountain the polka version of a famous commercial jingle wafted up. Jenny held him by the shoulders, staring into Monty's eyes.

"Maybe I'm not the most popular girl in Crosstown," she said, "but there's one thing I *do* know. If you go ahead and make that jump you're a coward."

He rolled his eyes, looking down to the giant sundae waiting in the distance.

"No, listen to me. You know you shouldn't make that jump. You aren't ready. But why do you want to do it? Because everyone expects you to. If you really need to prove you're a man, Monty, then quit right now. You want to show me you're brave? Give it up and let's go home."

"I never said I was brave." Monty shrugged. "I'm just here. I might as well do it." He pushed off with his poles, and sailed down the icy path to the forest.

Jenny called to him as he disappeared around a corner, but her voice faded with the distance. It didn't matter what she'd said, Monty had every one of Jenny's lessons constantly play-ing through his head. —Keep your skis together, bend your knees. Keep your knees together, don't get tense.

He tried to remember the course of the icy path, and he tried to remember how he'd acted when he skied down the first time, but it all happened so quickly. He zoomed past the rope and the torn police banner. Then he sailed on through the forest down to the outer slope.

When he broke through, Monty saw the whole expanse of Mount Maudlin. It stretched out before him like a great flat plain, tilted down to the earth. His skis scraped along the top of the ridge, then he sailed down the mountain, star-ing ahead with his eyes open wide.

Monty was moving even faster than before.

His skis began to vibrate, and the massive quarry pit opened up ahead like the Grand Canyon. He pressed hard on his outside foot, digging his pole into the snow to turn right. The edge of the quarry moved up on him at sixty miles an hour; even the noise of the skis was nothing compared to the sound of his heartbeat.

Monty nearly fell trying to turn, but he made it. Then suddenly he hit the metal sluice. It boomed like cannon fire as he raced down the length of it. Mr. Maudlin had a giant tin spoon attached to the outside of the sluice. Monty stared in wonder as he sailed off the edge, as his skis tapped the end of the spoon, as he toppled forward in a giant somersault, sixty feet over solid ground.

It happened in an instant. Monty saw the party down below, people staring in wonder. He saw one of his skis shooting away like a spear. There wasn't time to think about dying. With his one remaining ski, Monty tried to hold some sort of balance. To keep his balance he crouched as he sailed down onto the giant sundae, the crowd silently waiting for his accident. He kept his knees bent, his one ski beneath him, and he would have made the jump successfully, if it hadn't been for the fudge. A lump of the brown, industrial foam product stopped him short. His ski stuck right into it, and Monty sailed over the edge of the pool.

The last thing Monty saw before he blacked out was the open mouth of a tuba. He heard the first few beats of "Over the Rainbow," and then—nothing.

Monty woke up in the hospital, staring into Jenny's face. "You screwed up," she said, smiling.

"What happened?" He tried to move. It didn't work. There were pulleys and ropes around his lower torso.

"Well ..." Jenny began counting on her fingers. "First of all, your left ski flew off and went through the windshield of Laura's new car. She hates you now, by the way. Secondly, you broke the above-ground pool, the tuba, and your right leg."

"Wonderful," sighed Monty.

"But since you're still alive, I consider the jump a definite success." She patted his head affectionately. "And they named a dessert after you: Monty's Rocky Road. It's sort of a hot fudge sundae with a cherry on the side."

"Wonderful." Jenny pulled a newspaper from her backpack. Monty's picture was on the front page, caught in midair, legs spread wide, a look of horror on his face. "I guess I never really did know how to ski," he said softly.

"No, you did very well actually," she said, "for a beginner." Jenny placed a book in his lap: *Intermediate Skiing*, a training manual. "That leg will heal soon. Then I can start teaching you for real next year."